The Deep

The Deep

Mary Swan

a novella

The Porcupine's Quill

NATIONAL LIBRARY OF CANADA
CATALOGUING IN PUBLICATION DATA

Swan, Mary, 1953–
  The deep / Mary Swan.

ISBN 0-88984-248-5

I. Title.

PS8587.W344D44 2002   C813'.6   C2002-902157-X
PR9199.4S93D44 2002

1 2 3 4 • 04 03 02

Published by The Porcupine's Quill, www.sentex.net/~pql
68 Main Street, Erin, Ontario NOB ITO.

Based on an actual historical incident, all individuals and events
in this accounting are fictional.

Represented in Canada by the Literary Press Group.
Trade orders are available from University of Toronto Press.

We acknowledge the support of the
Ontario Arts Council, and the Canada
Council for the Arts for our publishing
program. The financial support of the
Government of Canada through the
Book Publishing Industry
Development Program is also
gratefully acknowledged.

For Linda, who found it

After

Here there are two tall windows, very tall, many-paned, and the gauzy white curtains swirl in the breeze, lift and fall like a breath, like a sigh. There is a faint, sweet smell, like blossoms; perhaps it is spring. The leaves on the trees also lift and sigh, all that can be seen through those windows. Sounds reach us from the street, wheels turning and hard shoes and sometimes a voice raised, calling out something, but they are muffled, all these sounds. Distant. Father told us once about the Queen's funeral, straw laid in the street to mute the sound. It is like that, and we wonder if someone has died.

How to Begin

Has it ever happened to you, that you have wakened suddenly from a long, deep sleep, that it takes some time for you to realize who you are, where you are? Familiar objects, even faces, become mysterious, remote. You stumble about, trailing the fog of sleep into the waking world, and nothing makes sense. Just a few, fuddled moments, if you're lucky. Until you splash your face with cold water and recognize it again, in the mirror above the basin. Until you drink a cup of tea, breathe fresh air, let routine tasks draw you back. Where do we go, in such a sleep, what is the world that we enter?

It may be France, in 1918.

Survival Suit

How to explain it, what it was like? The interview, and then
the notice that we were accepted, the official look of it, and
then the date for sailing, ten days on. A sudden twinge of
panic, of dismay – ten days, such an imaginable length of
time. So many things to do, to gather together, the
momentum of that carried us for a while. The vaccinations
and the endless lists. Blankets and heavy stockings and high
boots. Coats, thermos bottles, sewing case, flannel
nightgowns. Knife. Two closely written pages listing essential
equipment, with a note at the bottom reminding us that it
was our patriotic duty to bring as little luggage as possible.

We laughed about that when we went to dine with Miss
Reilly, and she told us how envious she was, how she wished
she were setting off too. We talked about the brave boys who
had given their lives, James, and the friends and brothers of
people we knew. And of course we reminisced about our
European journey, spoke of the spirit of France, of Belgium,
of how much we had learned. That time we stood in the little
church of San Maurizio, tears streaming down our faces, and
how no one thought it strange. Miss Reilly gave us each a slim
black pen that evening when we left, so that we would
remember to write her everything.

The next day, Father took us to lunch. Someone had told
him that the crossing was more dangerous than anything we'd
be close to in France, and so after we had eaten he insisted on
going with us to try on lifesaving suits. We saw the flicker in
his eye when the woman said that one suit could support
fourteen additional people hanging on to it. But then it was
gone and he said very firmly that we would require two suits.
To make him happy we tried them on all afternoon, although
it all seemed quite ridiculous. The heavy rubber suits, lined
with cork, the snapping steel clamps at chest and ankle,

buckling on the headgear. The woman showed us the special pockets, designed to hold bread and a flask of whisky, and assured us that along with the fourteen hangers-on, the suit would support the person wearing it for forty-eight hours in a standing position, submerged only to just above the waist. 'Ophelia!' we said together when we heard this, remembering the doll we had once. The flowers we braided in her long stiff hair and how we tried to float her in the shallow stream. How she kept bobbing up to stand, petals falling everywhere, until we finally tied our heavy wet stockings around her neck and then she did float, but face down. The trouble from Nan when she found us, not because of the stockings but because we'd been at the stream, and she hadn't known.

We left the store with two bulky parcels, and Father seemed quite relieved that he had been able to purchase what was required to keep us safe.

The Castle

Our mother was a sad woman lying on a couch, on a bed, or very occasionally wrapped in shawls and blankets in a chair on the veranda. We killed her, of course; everyone knew that.

We saw her every day, almost every day, though sometimes it was just a glimpse from the doorway. Her hazy face, eyes, amid the pillows in the darkened room. Nan holding our hands tightly, holding us back. Our mother's pale face shifting, swimming towards us through the gloom as she whispered, 'Hello, my darlings.'

'Hello, my darlings,' we mocked sometimes, laughing ourselves silly as we rolled in the soft grass, collecting stains that Nan would scold us for. And we whispered it at night, lying in our narrow beds, holding hands across the gulf between us. Goodnight, my darling. Goodnight, my darling.

Our mother had a smell, something flowery over something heavier, a little sweet. We recognized it in France, or something very like it. The smell of fear, of despair, of things slowly rotting.

Our brothers said that she had been beautiful. Tall with shining dark hair that she sometimes wore unpinned, and long silk dresses the colour of every flower in the garden. When they came home from school every few months they spent hours in her room, talking or reading to her; we heard their voices going on and on, with pauses where we imagined her own slipping in. They were much older than we were, down already forming on their upper lips, and it seemed a different world they described. Picnics and music and parties with candlelight, a cake shaped like a Swiss mountain and mounds of strawberries. These things they told us when we were older. When we were very small they despised us, could not be left alone with us, Nan said, for fear of what might happen.

Once we performed for our mother, turning somersaults and something we called cartwheels all over the front lawn. And as we spun and rolled we heard a sound we didn't recognize; we stood, finally, looking up at the veranda, panting a little and brushing the hair out of our eyes. In her chair, from the midst of her blankets and shawls, our mother was laughing. She laughed until she cried, until she could hardly catch her breath, and then we stood, resting our heads near her lap, and she stroked our hair and said, 'Oh, my dears, it wasn't meant to be this way.'

So we understood that we were all under a spell. Crawling through the tangled vines in the kitchen garden we imagined them growing and growing, twining round the big stone house, blotting out the sun, growing thick and fast over the windows of the room where the princess lay sleeping for a hundred years. Jameson roared when we started to hack our way through, so we became more cautious, sitting in a sunny corner popping pods of stolen peas and imagining the prince, the white horse he would ride upon. How he would sweep Jameson aside and slash his way through the jungle with his sharp sword and ride through the big front door, up the curving stairs, leave his horse grazing in the hallway while he rescued the sleeping princess. Then there would be a feast with a thousand candles blazing; she would wear a long sea-green gown shot with silver, and laugh and dance with the prince until morning.

The prince had blue eyes and long fair hair. Years later we found a photograph of our father as a very young man; the face was exactly what we had imagined and we were amazed, for we would never have cast our father as the prince. Or would we? Had we, perhaps, been shown that picture before, and what did that mean? We talked about that for hours, warming our toes before the stove while a dark rain slashed at the windows, but we reached no conclusion.

* * *

Our father also had a smell; he brought it with him from the city. Cigars and dust and ashes. As children we grew prickly in his presence, longing to hurl things about, to stick out our tongues, to do something shocking. But terrified too, of saying the wrong thing.

We saw him in his study usually, before we went to bed. The shadowed room, his face lit strangely from the lamp on the desk, the piles of papers and folders and a thin curl of cigar smoke. We assumed that he blamed us too, and wished we had never been. He asked us if we had been good, if we had done all our lessons, and of course we said yes. And then he called us to him, we walked around the sides of the desk and he circled an arm about our shoulders, planted a kiss on our foreheads, first one, then the other, the scratchy tickle of his moustache. He never called us by our names and we never tried to fool him as we did everyone else. It would have been pointless, for we were sure he didn't know or care which was which.

When we talked about it later, those long nights when the guns went on and on, we wondered if it was just that he didn't know quite what to do with us. He had no sister, no other daughters; he may have been just ill at ease. And busy, of course. Certainly when we were older he would talk to us, ask us what we were reading or studying, he seemed to know things which, looking back through a rainy night, suggested that he watched us, thought about us. If our mother had been there perhaps – but of course that was the whole point.

15

The Corporal Remembers

They made me think of horses – well, they would, wouldn't they? Skittish white horses, dream horses, maybe. You know how they raise their hooves, their legs, holding them in the air, trying so hard to become weightless, not touch the ground. I can't explain. But that's what they made me think of. That's all.

The Fountain

There is a portrait of our mother; it hangs in our father's
study, a dark room even on the brightest of days. The artist
stayed in our house while he worked on it, and Nan still talks
with some surprise about how he made her laugh. And there
is another picture, done at the same time. A quick, light
sketch in soft colours that used to hang by the fire, until our
father let Marcus take it away to his own house.

In this second picture our mother wears a pale yellow dress
and sits on the edge of a fountain. James and Marcus are two
young boys in shades of blue, sitting on either side, all of
them looking down at something she holds in her lap. From
the position, from the shape of her mouth, her half-parted
lips, it looks as if she is reading them a story, though it seems
a strange place to do that. We used to love that picture when
we were young, used to stare and stare at it. The grass so
exactly the colour of rich, late spring grass and the way he
painted the spray from the fountain, a glistening in the air. It
hung on the wall by the fire like a window to another world
and it seemed quite possible that by staring hard enough we
could step right through.

There is a signature in the bottom corner of that painting,
and a date. When we were older we realized from that date
that we were already growing, beneath the pale yellow dress,
getting ready to smash that world to pieces.

The fountain doesn't exist any longer; the space where it
stood holds a circular bed of flowers that change with the
seasons. We caused that too. When we were very small, two at
the most, the silly girl who helped care for us fell asleep
beneath a shady tree. We don't remember her; they say we
can't remember any of it, we were far too young. But we do
remember, we are certain that we do. The prismed spray of

the fountain, the sound and feel of it. Like the feeling, not
just the thought, of being hand in hand. The way the water
was neither hot nor cold but just the temperature to welcome
us in. It wasn't deep, but we were very small and it was deep
enough to close over our heads. And we remember the magic
of underwater, the absolute silence and peace. It's not likely
there were fish in that fountain, but we remember the colour,
darting streaks of light.

We must somehow have pulled each other out, though
when we think of how it was inside, we wonder why.
Clambered back over the side and began to walk, walking
ahead of our wet footprints toward the big house where a
door was already opening, a white shape running. Walking
hand in hand toward everything that came after.

This happened on a bright day in June. We know that;
we've been told. So why do we have another picture in our
minds, just as clear? The grass brown and dead, trees bare
except for a few withered curls of leaf that rattle when the
wind comes. Two people, large and dark, with dark heavy
feet, carry two small bodies, held forward in their arms like
an offering about to be deposited on a stone. Water drips fron
the sky, and from the sodden bundles, and there is a vast
silence.

Mrs Moore

They were angels. And by that I don't just mean they were good, although they were that. Kind and hardworking, generous with their time and their money. Not minding what they did. I had my doubts, when I first met them. Even bedraggled as they were from the journey, it was clear they'd not done a hard day's work in their lives. And we'd had a few like that – not many, but a few who couldn't take it. Who had some vision of themselves passing plates of cucumber sandwiches or wheeling some handsome boy about the garden. Garden! And there were some, of course, who were there for a good time – well, why not, I said. As long as they did their work, as long as they were there when I needed them, what business of mine was it?

Listen to me now – I would have shocked myself speechless a few years ago. But those poor boys, the look in their eyes and their poor broken bodies, the way they twitched and jumped, but always ready with a joke, with a smile. And some of the women – well, they wouldn't have much of a chance would they, otherwise, if I tell the truth. Which makes you wonder, doesn't it, just what it takes for a fellow to overlook thick ankles, a crossed eye. Like I said, as long as I could count on them to be where they should, to do their work, as long as they didn't get themselves diseased or worse and become a problem – well, who am I to say they shouldn't take some pleasure while they could?

Not that the twins were like that, nothing like. If anything, they were a bit too much the other way. Too serious, you know, and I don't think they'd had much to do with men in their lives. Not romantically, I mean. There was a young fellow they went around with, for a while. I don't know what was in it, just friendly, I would imagine. My friend Dr Thomas told me the boy was having a course of treatment – you know.

Like so many. Although usually it was the French girls to blame for that and this boy didn't look – well, he didn't look like he'd ever be looking for companionship, if you know what I mean. He looked like he could be choosy. Though the way things were over there I suppose that's no guarantee. Not if half the things my friend the Colonel says are true.

So this boy – I can't think of his name right now, but he was a devil all right. And such a joker – he had a gift for that. No matter what kind of mood you were in when you ran into him, you'd be laughing by the time he moved on. He wasn't in our camp too long, a couple of weeks, maybe. Though he'd pop up every once in a while after, to see the twins. And that charm of his worked on them too, you could tell. They were lighter, somehow, when he was around. Like I say though, I don't know what was in it. I'd never really known any twins, not really known, until I met Esther and Ruth. And they were just like you'd imagine twins to be, if you had to imagine. Same voice, same expressions, moved the same way. And always *we* – I'd forgotten that, I guess I got so used to it. We did this, we think that, never *I*. After a time they started wearing different-coloured ribbons around their wrists, so people could tell them apart, but I always had the feeling they used to switch those around every once in a while, like some private little joke. Or maybe it just didn't matter to them. I used to wonder sometimes – I mean it's bad enough if two friends fall for the same young man, especially if he's a bit of a scoundrel like that one. It seems I heard he was wounded, just at the end of the war, or had some trouble, but I don't remember just what it was. Ah well, it's all water under the bridge – oh Lordy, I didn't mean to say that.

The Headmistress

I

There will be those who think it is somehow my fault. Not say it, perhaps, but think it. Their father may. He came to see me in my office, sat in the green chair, refused a cup of tea. And asked me to persuade them not to go, and never to tell them that he had asked. 'You have influence,' he said. 'They would listen to you, to what you say.'

At the time I told him I had no right to do that. That they were grown women, twenty-six years old, that they had to make their own decisions. I pretended, and I see now that it was pretending, that I didn't know what he meant by *influence*. As if I'd never said any of the things I've said, lived the life I've lived. He recognized the pretence, that showed for a moment behind his gold spectacles. But all he said was, 'Very well.' And we talked of general things until he left. We have always just missed saying things to each other, their father and I.

It is cold out tonight and a vicious sleet smashes against the window. But I sit here by the fire, quite warm and dry, a tray close at hand, my books, my pen. And it comes to me that all the things I've said and done, all the battles fought have been from this position of warmth and comfort. This morning at the school I looked down on those rows of upturned faces and thought that they receive my message from the same position of comfort. No fault of theirs, but what about mine?

I believed I was sending them into the world well equipped, year after year, a generation of women proud of their minds, secure in their worth, who believed in truth, in beauty, who would spread that belief by their very existence. I believed that the world would have to become a better place, that they would see to it. Perhaps I should have given them armour. Taught them to think but not to feel, taught them to save themselves. I say this in all seriousness.

I have said that we always seemed to just miss saying things, their father and I. Now I have to stop and think about that. I met him first almost fifteen years ago; I have known him longer than I knew my own parents. We were interviewing each other, I suppose, about the possibility of the girls attending the school. I had been to a meeting outside and was taking the tram back through an unfamiliar part of the city. I remember that I was a little worried about being late, that I was in that state of heightened awareness that comes when your surroundings are strange, when you must actually use your eyes and ears. The streets, the houses we skimmed by were like those I knew, and yet not. The people getting on and off like that too. As if a glass had shifted to distort, ever so slightly. Like those moments in a dream when little things are just odd enough to make you wonder if you *are* dreaming. It was summer, the trees in full dark leaf, and a steady rain fell from a sky that was a vast, washed grey. The tram was a little cocoon moving through it, and the people who pulled themselves on from outside were giddy with the rain, but gently so. Some soaked to the skin, wiping water from their hands and cheeks. A middle-aged woman scattering droplets from her black umbrella as she closed it, laughing as she caught her breath and saying things to herself that would have had us looking carefully away at any other time or place. But it was clear, there, that it was rain madness, nothing more. We were all touched with it.

That was what I came from, the day I first met their father. Still worried about the time, I hurried down the corridor to my new office, lit the lamps, sent for tea. I was expecting the tea when the soft tap at the door came, and was quite taken aback when a grey-haired man walked into my room. He

22

looked like what he was, a successful man of business, yet there was something hesitant about the way he crossed the threshold, something that made me want immediately to put him at ease. I remember that he told me right away that his wife was dead. I knew that, of course, and knew that she had been for a number of years, and I thought it strange that he would mention it like that. But then I remembered who he was, his reputation in the world of business, and realized that it was probably deliberate, some kind of tactic. First words, after all, can be just as calculated as the clothing we put on, the faces we compose to meet someone or to face the world.

Mr A went on to tell me that his sons had gone away to school from the beginning, but that he had always wished to keep his daughters, then eleven, at home. That from all he had found out it seemed that my school would provide the type of education he wished them to have, with the added advantage of being only a short train ride from their home, so that they could attend as day pupils. 'They're clever girls,' he said, 'but a little –'

There was another tap at the door, really the tea this time, and we fussed about with cups and tiny spoons. He drank his clear, as I usually do, but for some reason that day I added milk and sugar to my cup. The lights pushed the rain-coloured air to the corners of the room and I remember thinking that it was another cocoon, like the tram. This circle of light where we sat, the music of silver spoons.

'They don't really know other children,' he said, after lifting his cup to his lips. 'We live a very quiet life where we are. And they seem quite content, but I've been thinking.... Also, they are growing up, you see ...' 'Of course,' I said, and then he said, 'I was born a twin myself, but my brother didn't survive,' and while I was wondering what to say to that he took off his glasses and rubbed at his left eye, saying, 'How strange, I don't think I've ever told anyone that.'

I didn't believe him, thinking it was another part of some

23

peculiar strategy. The same way he showed his face, vulnerable without the spectacles.

As it happened, at that particular time we were rather desperate for new pupils, but I had learned a few tricks myself. I suggested that he come back with the girls, bringing a sample of the work they were currently doing. Told him that although we usually had a long waiting list, there was a possibility that we could accept them both for the fall term.

How much of it is my fault? Or because of my influence, which comes to the same thing. Those letters they wrote, my responses. Before they stopped writing. You see, I thought what they needed was reassurance. That they were doing the right thing, that it was all worthwhile. And I believed that it was, it's not that I lied. But reading their letters again I can't believe that I was so blind; my whole being cringes when I think of the letters I wrote back.

Am I too hard on myself? It's true that it's only now that so many have returned, telling their stories, now that we see who has become rich, or richer, what the world is still like, only now that it's all so clear. But I failed them, there's no escaping that. What they told me was not what I myself believed, and instead of listening I tried to nudge them back to my way. So much for all those fine words about confidence and identity. I failed them, and now they're dead.

Many years ago I knew a young man who died of a fever in Africa. If I had agreed to marry him he would not have gone to Africa, would not have caught the fever, would not have died. But I did not agree, because I was already taking the first steps along what I believed was my proper path. Because I believed that in marrying him I would have lost control of my life, and even though I still think that was true, I am no longer so certain that it would have been the worst thing. After the death of my parents I was raised by an aunt and uncle. They were ignorant people; things happened in that house that I have not told a soul. My parents had left a little money for my education, and I understood that this would be my means of escape, my way of saving myself. I know that I didn't kill him, that earnest young man whose face I can no longer recall. A fever killed him. But it can't be denied that I played a part. As with Ruth and Esther. I remember that first day when their father took off his glasses and rubbed at his eye, and I realize suddenly that I could talk to him about this, that he is perhaps the only person I could talk to about this. Except for the fact that he is the last person in the world I could talk to about this.

Sailing

We stood at the railing, looking down at the mass of people, and just as we spotted our father he took off his hat and waved it frantically in the air. We had never known him to do such a thing. We were too far away to see anything more than the dark overcoat, the pale blob that was his face, his hand clutching the waving black hat. But we were struck by an astonishing thought. It was as if we were really seeing him. Over that distance, in the midst of all the noise and confusion, we saw something completely unexpected. Our father moved slowly always, deliberately, and we realized that we pictured him motionless, like a photograph. Sitting at his desk in a pool of light, or at the dinner table. Even at the wheel of his new motor car, he was somehow still while the machine hurtled through space. We remembered how he ran up the stairs the day our mother died, how we had no idea he could move so fast. The very air, after he had rushed past, was shivering and charged. The same thing now, in the frenzied waving of his hat. As if something had burst from him, alone in the crowd on the dock.

A girl stood beside us at the rail, a girl with very blue eyes and pale hair tucked under a funny little hat, made from the same material as her coat. When our eyes met she gave a little smile and said, 'I don't know why I'm looking down, there's no one here to see me off.' Then she turned and walked quickly away, leaving us wondering whether we should follow. But then the ship began to move, and we watched the land fall away, imagining, long after it was possible, that we still saw the black speck of our father's waving hat.

We told ourselves that it was no different from any other crossing. There were uniforms, or course, and a disproportionate number of young people on board, but we had been to Europe twice before; it was not, we said, as if we were going into something completely unfamiliar. What can have been in our minds?

The girl's name was Elizabeth; we shared a table with her at dinner that first night, and came to know her well on the voyage. It was not difficult to know her well; we had never met a person who talked so freely, so openly. We learned very quickly that she was going overseas to find her brother. Arthur, his name was. Art. He was nineteen, just a little more than two years younger than she was, and he had gone over as an ambulance driver just after his eighteenth birthday. They hadn't heard from him in five or six months and her mother was terribly worried. And she had enough to worry about without that, poor Mother, with Elizabeth's father being so sick and four younger ones at home, such a little bit of money to live on. So they held a family meeting one night in the kitchen, and decided that Elizabeth should volunteer, so she could be over there and find out where he was, how he was. Her mother was tormented by the thought that he was in a hospital somewhere, alone and suffering, missing them. The other possibility she didn't allow anyone to mention.

Elizabeth had already taken a nursing course; she got interested when her father became ill, so she was accepted without any problem. Someone had told her not to mention Art when she went to be interviewed, so she didn't, although she felt terrible keeping it back. Somehow her mother found the money to get most of the things she needed to take with her, and she made her a new coat and hat out of an overcoat that her father wouldn't wear again. But there was nothing left over for anyone to travel with her to the city, so she had to say goodbye at the station and she missed them all so; she'd never spent a night away from home before.

We pictured it all as Elizabeth talked, pictured it as a scene from a sentimental novel, so removed from our own experience. The scrubbed table in the warm kitchen, the dishes cleared away and the kettle simmering on the stovetop. All of them there except Father, whose coughing could be heard from upstairs. Mother looking so tired, her hands swollen and chapped. Young Bob, who was trying desperately to grow a moustache. He thought he should be the one to go, thought he could just lie about his age, but Mother said absolutely not, and besides, she needed him so much at home. Bob was fourteen and growing almost as quickly as he thought he was. Nessie thought she should go too, so Elizabeth wouldn't be all alone, but they needed the money she brought in, and she didn't have the nursing course so they didn't think she'd have much luck trying to go on her own. Peter and Amy were too young but they were there, Amy sitting on her red cushion, watching and listening. When it was all decided, Elizabeth and her mother went upstairs to tell Father, but he fell asleep before they'd finished.

We didn't tell Elizabeth much about our own family, talking instead about things we'd heard about the war, about our European journeys, about France, the last time we saw it. About red-roofed villages and the quiet of the countryside, small cobbled squares. The food in Paris, the gardens and museums and galleries. We told all this to Elizabeth, who cheerfully said that she didn't know a thing about art, but perhaps she'd have a chance to learn. What else could we have told Elizabeth that would not have seemed grotesque to her? That we'd heard our mother laugh once? That our father bought us rubber suits and waved his hat as we sailed away? That our brother Marcus didn't see us off, not because he couldn't afford to, but because he had a business luncheon. We couldn't tell her about James, for obvious reasons, but even if we had, she couldn't have understood how it was. Perhaps it was because our brothers were so much older, because they went away to school, because they were cruel to us when we were young. Perhaps that was why they didn't seem connected to us, like the most casual of acquaintances.

When we heard that James had been killed we were sad, but
in a strangely abstract way. Like hearing about the brother of
someone you went to school with, or met at a dance. It was
different for Marcus, of course, and for our father. The light
burning in his study until morning, a smell of whisky on
occasion.

After James enlisted he came home to collect some things
and we were alone in the house one afternoon. Rain fell
outside the tall windows and the rooms were chill; we had a
fire lit and sat reading beside it. And James came in, restless,
pacing about the room. Touching pictures, the vase on the
mantel, a dish on the table. He was a little stocky, James, his
oiled hair thinning already, his chin very square and his eyes
pale. We saw suddenly that he would look very like our
father, when he reached his age.

Finally James stopped pacing and drew another chair
closer to the fire, sat drumming the fingers of his right hand
on his knee. We closed our books and asked him something –
when he would sail, likely, or if he had everything he needed.
And he answered, and then began to talk about others he
knew who were going at the same time, or had already sailed.
How he couldn't wait to be there in the thick of it, whipping
the Hun, all those phrases that came so easily to everyone's
lips in those days. 'Poor Marcus,' he said. 'He'll miss all the
fun.'

And then, being James, he went on and on about what a
lot of fools the generals were, how they were doing it all
wrong, how what was needed was – well, we didn't really
listen, we'd heard it all before. He got up to put another log
on the fire and burned his finger arranging it. We looked up
at his exclamation and saw him put his finger in his mouth
for a moment and we noticed, at the same moment, that his
eyes were glistening in the firelight, that there were tears in
his pale eyes. And one of us said, 'Are you afraid, James?' It
was a moment to ask and be answered, and he took his finger

from his mouth, looked at it and said, 'Oh yes.'

That was all; the next moment he strode over to draw the heavy curtains against the fading day, and left the room. Then back to camp, then onto a ship, then marching down a dark, rutted road on the way to the trenches for the first time. The scream of a shell, and nothing more.

We tell ourselves that it is too easy to call a moment by a crackling fire the true moment. To say that the glint of tears was more real than the childhood cruelty, the adult arrogance and bluster. Our brother James was not particularly likeable, and meant little to us. Nor did we mean much to him. Our sadness when he died was more because that was so. A moment in a rainy room was just one of the things we remembered, when we happened to think of him. We knew that this would have been incomprehensible to Elizabeth, perhaps appalling.

But is it true, what we've said about James? What we felt, what we didn't feel? Is it possible that it was really like that, all our life before? So removed. Or does it just seem so from here? Here where things are so different, where what we think about is just the cocoa, will it hold out, and where can we get some eggs? How much our feet hurt, the long soak we will give them, if we can get hot water. Will our headache ever go, can we stand it another hour, two, the noise and the heat and the pounding. Will this one ever come back, or that one.

Walking back to the hut one grey afternoon, boards over mud that was almost frozen and so quiet, suddenly, the canteen left behind. The sky heavy, air cold and dense with the rain that had fallen, would fall again. By the tree that we called the last tree in Europe, Hugh sat writing. He had a wooden chair he'd scrounged somewhere, a couple of boards laid over some empty tins. He was wearing a grey sweater, the colour of dense smoke, pearled with moisture from the air, holes in one elbow. Black pipe clenched between his teeth, smoke, more grey, wisping up. We were on our way to sleep a little, thinking of nothing but the chill in our bones, how wonderful it was to walk through such silence to a damp cot, to wrap the blankets tight, close eyes. We were happy with that, at that moment. Wanted nothing more from life, and the sight of Hugh in his smoke-coloured sweater became all entwined with that moment of perfect contentment.

The Headmistress

II

Mr A brought the girls to meet me a week later. I was sleeping better by then; the day was sunny and warm and I felt calm and quite like myself, none of the eeriness surrounding our first meeting. It's difficult – I came to know them well over many years, or thought I did, and so it's difficult to look back to that first meeting, clear of any of the knowledge or familiarity that came later. What struck me first, I think, was their calmness. They were not especially beautiful children, but there was something very appealing about them. Their long hair was tied back neatly and although they weren't dressed identically, that was somehow the impression they gave. When they were not responding to one of my questions they both looked down at their polished shoes, the toes just brushing the floor. This did not seem like shyness, or deference. Rather it was as if they returned to some serious and self-contained contemplation. They replied politely to anything I asked, whichever one answered speaking in the plural. I'd quite forgotten that, but I remember how it struck me at the time. The way they never spoke together, but there was no hesitation, no collision, conversation flowing easily from one or the other so that the effect was of talking to a single person.

It's an interesting exercise, this recollection, the way it makes you remember more and more. Like opening a door, having no control over who walks through. Since I heard the news I've been looking at photographs. Ones from that European trip, several that they sent me from Paris, in their uniforms. But it wasn't until after the memorial service that I made myself bring out the oldest. I suppose it was seeing everyone there, all the old pupils. A year or two after they came to the school we received an unexpected bequest, and decided to use part of it to make a proper photographic record, of the rooms, of the teachers and pupils. At the end of the year I gave each one a small, individual portrait in a soft leather folder.

The photographer we hired was a very talented young man, several years younger than myself. Jones, his name was, and he had a soft Welsh voice to go with it. He went west later and I don't know what happened to him. But we had several long conversations about art, about photography and painting. I would have thought, if I had thought about it at all, that photography was a scientific process, a way of recording reality, would have thought that was the marvel of it. But Mr Jones made me see it differently. He said, for example, that while a painter has all kinds of tricks at his disposal – different materials, different brushes and brushstrokes, all the colours of the rainbow – a photographer works only with light and shadow. This particular conversation took place in an empty classroom; there was a wild blue sky through the tall windows, the tops of flame-coloured trees.

'This moment,' Mr Jones said, 'were I to photograph it – the record of reality would be a man and a woman talking in an empty room. Now if I were a painter, of course, I could add things. The colour of that sky, the leaves, and I could pick up that colour at the throat of your dress, perhaps a touch on your cheekbones. I could change your expression slightly, or my own, the curve of your lips, and the painting would not be about an empty room.

'But what can I do with my camera? Oh, there are some tricks of course. Those photographs for your booklet – there are ways to make rooms look bigger, the view more enticing. But how do I photograph a moment, this moment, say, and have it clear that the leaves outside the window are not the soft green of spring, that the year is dying and not beginning?

I must pull out the truth of it, of a person or a place. If there is to be anything real, I must draw out the heart.'

I don't remember what happened next, but there was truth in what he said, and the photographs are the proof. I have them all together in a folder, a record of a particular year of my life.

Mr Jones spent a great deal of time in the school that autumn. He was clearly an artist and not a businessman, for he was paid one price to provide photographs of each teacher and pupil, yet he took some again and again until he was satisfied, going away with the plates and coming back to try once more. In his studio he showed me the different attempts, laying them out on a round table covered with a rich blue cloth, and I understood what he meant.

Of course, he had more tricks than he admitted. I observed all the individual sittings; it would not have been proper otherwise, even in 1905. I saw the way he arranged the light or the folds of a dress, positioned the arms. The way the sitter submitted totally, becoming somehow inanimate while he moved limbs, smoothed the hair, turned the chin just a fraction. Called for different props – a book, a flute, a flower. But the end result, trick or not, was as he had said. Some essence of the women and girls I knew, captured in a way that was quite astounding. In the end it was only the twins who gave him trouble. He came back for them again and again, all through that cold, dark December, until finally he admitted defeat and posed them together.

My own photograph from that time both pleases and disturbs me. I remember every sitting vividly, at the school and in his studio, yet I can't imagine a moment when I looked like this. I know I faced the camera straight on, unafraid, yet my eyes somehow slide off, away from it. My hair is dressed as I have always worn it, yet it seems to be struggling to escape. Wisps worked free to dance along my cheek, to wave in the soft light about my head. My hands are folded as I remember, but there is a tension in the fingers, and the bottom hand is slightly blurred, as if caught in a sudden movement. And I am certain my mouth never looked like this. The photograph pleases me, as a work of art might; it invites one to understand certain things about the woman in it. But I have never recognized it as myself.

Letter

Dear Father,

Thank you so much for your latest package, which arrived
safely two days ago. We are greedily devouring the books and
chocolate, and the stockings are a godsend. Please thank
Janet – we assume she bought them – and tell her how glad
we are to get them, as what we brought is much be-darned.
We were very sorry to hear about John Tupper.

You ask where we are – of course we can't say exactly, but
can tell you that we are fairly close to the front, but not in any
danger. This is a sort of interim camp, for men on their way to
or from the front. Sometimes they go from here to a real rest
camp, or sometimes right back up to the line. When we first
came here we stayed in a tent pitched on the stubble field
behind the camp. Very damp and cold. But just last week we
moved into a room made from an old storeroom in the end of
the canteen hut. Small, but it seems like a palace to us after
the tent. We have just enough room for our two cots with their
now-dry straw mattresses and our trunks, and one of the boys
pounded some nails into the walls so we can hang up our tin
hats, gas masks and clothes. We also have a little stove, but
don't need to use it much now that the nights are not so cold.
The hills round about are covered with wildflowers this time
of year, and in our free time if we are not sleeping – which we
seem to do a great deal of – we take lovely long walks.

As you see, we are well settled in and the routine of our
days no longer seems at all strange. We generally mess with
the officers, and the food is plentiful, though not particularly
satisfying. Mornings we spend washing hundreds of mugs
from the previous night in the canteen, and preparing
sandwiches and sometimes cakes and sweets for the afternoon
and evening. Two little French boys keep us supplied with

wood for the small stove, which is all we have to heat the huge kettles of cocoa and coffee that we go through each day. In addition to ourselves and Mrs Moore, who is in charge, a woman named Berthe from the nearby village helps out. She speaks no English and as Mrs Moore knows no French we do a great deal of translating and thank heaven for those classes at Miss Reilly's. We had a letter from her last week and she mentioned that she saw you at dinner at the Barretts'. It is so strange sometimes to think of life going on at home, just like before. You would be amazed at the life we have settled into here, but settled in we have. The work is hard and might be seen as monotonous, but we know it's important, the boys so appreciative of any little thing we do for them. There are always a few who can barely read or write, and if there's time we often write letters to their dictation. And mend torn shirts or sew on stripes or badges. All kinds of little things that mean a great deal over here. We can't, as we said, tell you where we are, but we are close enough to hear the guns. Don't worry though, we have been assured that the camp will move if the fighting draws much closer.

There is a large hospital in a beautiful old chateau a few miles from here, and on our free day we usually go there to do what we can to help out. We read to the soldiers or write more letters, help feed those that need help. The nurses are wonderful but so busy; they are always glad to see us. So you see our days are very full and we really have no time to miss home, so you mustn't worry about that. We must close now as it is very late and we will be rising with the sun.

Stain

When our mother actually died, you would have thought we would all have been prepared for it. Living her half-life for years. Off in her upstairs room the last long time, just a hint of recognition in her sunken eyes, and that only sometimes. You would have thought that we would have gotten on with our lives, that she would have been a sad, fixed point outside our orbit. What we would have thought at the time, if we had to explain it. For our father too, who rarely saw her, as far as we knew, who enquired after her health, her day, when the nurse sat down to eat with us, as one would of a mutual acquaintance.

It was Sunday morning. Early June, that time of year when the sky is blue every time you open your eyes, when the lilac blossoms fill the air. The night nurse was having a cup of tea in the kitchen, talking about carrots and peas, and we were just coming through the door, blinking after the light outside, our shoes wet with dew.

And then someone cried out, and we ran too; ahead of us the door of the study flung open, our father with his shirt sleeves caught up, running up the stairs, we'd never seen him move like that. The gold pen falling from his hand to roll and rattle, a small distinct noise amid the calls, the sound of thumping feet. Mrs B coming after, stooping to pick it up automatically, not even looking, slipping it into her apron pocket where it continued to ooze. The dark, spreading stain on her apron pocket – it seemed that stain spread out slowly to cover our whole lives.

Marcus

They were always strange, always trouble. From the very beginning, when they took our mother away. We were called home from school to see her before she died, although as it happened her dying took years. But those days we were home when the house was hushed and strange we would hear their thin squalling in the night. James thought we should kill them, and we tried a few times, I don't remember how, childish things I'm sure, but someone always stopped us. In the end we were glad to go back to school.

As they grew up they stopped squalling of course, and took to whispering, heads together. The sound of a couple of snakes. They had their own language for a while, a lot of nonsense words that they seemed to understand completely. The day of Mother's funeral they sliced themselves up with broken glass and had to be carried upstairs, screaming and kicking and getting blood everywhere. And how glad James and I were to hear them screaming even louder while Nan and Mrs B scrubbed their wounds with alcohol. When Father sent us up to the nursery later they were sitting up in bed with their legs all bandaged, eating cake, looking pale and oh so smug.

The War Book

It began to seem, after a time, that everyone had something. Had one thing that they'd seen or heard, that they couldn't shake off, that they carried, would carry forever, like a hard, dull stone in the heart. Not obvious things, not blood and mayhem, for that was everywhere and there was nothing exceptional about that. But it might be the shell of a house, seen through a train window. A little place, in what was left of a village they passed by, part of two walls left standing and a mess of rubble inside. It might lead to an obsessive need to discover – or maybe just to wonder – what was the name of the village, and who had lived in that house, what had happened, what *exactly* had happened to them. Or it might be a rope swing, still hanging from a blasted tree, the line of a little girl's neck in an echoing black station, one half of a beautiful bowl. A woman in black whacking the backside of a crying child all along a deserted street. Why was the child crying? Not that there weren't reasons enough to cry, but what was it, at just that moment? Or a creased photograph found somewhere, no way to know anything about the people in it, not even what side they were on. A white cat sleeping in a patch of sunlight, a piece of music heard in a most unlikely place. We thought if we could gather those things together we would call it 'The War Book'. And that would be the only way to communicate it, to give someone an idea of how it was.

Hugh's story concerned his friend Tom, the one he grew up with, joined up with. They'd stayed together, against all the odds, and one frosty morning they were standing together on the fire step and Hugh saw something glittering in the frozen mud at his feet. He bent to pick it up; his fingers were numb and he fumbled at it, cursed. 'What?' Tom said, turning his head, looking down at the spot where Hugh crouched. And then with a thud he was lying with his dead eyes looking *up*

at the spot where Hugh crouched, the glittering object
between his fingers, and Hugh remembers looking at it, seeing
that it was only a jagged bit of wood, something that could
never have glittered at all.

So Hugh's story is about mathematics, about physics,
about how he tried to work it all out. The chances of the
sniper's bullet finding that exact spot at the base of Tom's ear.
The distance to the other side, and if the bullet had already
left the gun when Hugh suddenly crouched. He drew
diagrams, tried to work out exactly where the other had been,
how tall he was, what he looked like. Did he squeeze the
trigger slowly, or with a sudden burst of excitement? He
called on everything he'd learned in that school a world away,
smell of chalk dust in his nostrils, the way it looked, floating
in the sunlight through the high windows, the creak of his
desk chair, the oiled floor. He knew he hadn't paid enough
attention – he'd usually copied Tom's assignments, after all.
But he thought he could learn what he needed to know.

And he thought about all the things that could have made
a difference. If he hadn't seen the glittering thing that
couldn't possibly have glittered, he and Tom would have
remained standing exactly as they were, the bullet would have
thumped into the wall of the trench behind them, between
them, or maybe not come at all. Or the sniper himself – if
he'd had to scratch his nose suddenly, if someone had called
to him or some noise made him look away, only for an
instant. If he'd had a cut on his finger, making it a little stiff,
if his eyelashes had been longer, his vision blurred for an
instant.

When that kind of thinking drove him mad, he would
think instead about the bullet. The place where it was made –
gloomy, he pictured it, and very noisy. Heat and sparks flying.
The long journey it made even to get to the fingers that
loaded it into the gun. All the things that could have changed
it, even then. The temperature that morning, so clear and

cold and no wind, but what if there had been? Or not even a wind but some shift, some tiny shift in the currents of air, the last breath of some storm that whirled around a mountain somewhere, the disturbance of someone running, even a cough. If someone had coughed in Paris – one of us, say, we were there. If one of us had coughed in Paris at exactly the right moment, would Tom still be alive?

Rain

So tired tonight, too tired to do anything, even to order
scattered thoughts. Silent except for the rain that splatters
against the window, against the flimsy walls of the hut,
splatters fitfully, as if tossed by a bored child. Think of the
rain falling here, how it must be falling all over the country,
all the way to the coast, to the grim Atlantic. Roiling there, a
tumbled picture in black and white, the winds that toss those
waves driving the rain on. Only in that deep, wintry zone far
beneath is everything still and silent, suspended in dark green
light. But up above the rain sweeps on, rolls over another
shore. Splatters like this against the windows of our old room,
but the room is empty, we are not there. And even if we were
to return it would be empty; quite impossible, now, for us to
be there.

In His Study the Father Closes His Eyes

And thinks about what he has lost. It is very quiet and, although his children were never noisy, he knows that this is the silence of their absence, that it will be like this for the rest of his life.

He will sell the house, of course. The big house in the country, bought with the first of his money. The place where the happy life was to be lived. How can it be that they're all gone? Alice. James. Esther and Ruth. His daughters brushed his cheek with their cool lips, first one and then the other. First Esther, with the slightly higher arch to her eyebrow, and then Ruth. The ship waited, a big, hard lump of the inevitable. He waved like a madman, swept off his hat and waved that too, long after it began to move away. Thinking that if he stopped at all he would snap the fragile thread, that they would lose sight of the place they must come back to and gently drift away forever. His shoulder ached for days, and he welcomed it.

Marcus is not gone, of course, Marcus is still alive. In his rooms in the city, surrounded by furniture no longer needed in the big house, and by his own things from when he was a boy. The painting of the happy life hangs near Marcus's bed, where the father need never see it. Marcus is still alive, still in the business, still making money. And he might still marry, have children who will run and jump and tumble, the juice of different fruits smeared on their chins.

Could they belong to Marcus, these ghost children who flicker behind his eyes? Marcus, the pale second son, the one who was always there, just there, two steps behind James, even when he grew to be the taller. What does Marcus feel, suddenly an only child? They meet in the office or outside it, with sheaves of paper or without, and there is an amazing harmony, the way they think about the business, the way it

lives for them, what they see in its future. The war years have
been good for them, very good, and the father wonders if
Marcus also feels guilty at the way he can't help being pleased
with that. Excited by that. Distracted from his grief.

Perhaps they do belong to Marcus, the ghost children
whose running footsteps patter along the floors above his
head. Perhaps Marcus will meet the right woman and find
himself a completely different life. But the father remembers
that he himself found the right woman, that it guaranteed
nothing but this long night alone in the creaking house.

And there was Anne Reilly, the girls' headmistress. A
handsome woman, intelligent and witty. Comfortable with
children. She would have looked just right, through
candlelight, at the end of the table. In all his encounters with
her over the years there had been this flutter of possibility.
But he could never get to it, through the thicket of their first
meeting. He had been expecting an older woman, although
she was, at the time, older than he first assumed. When he
opened the door she was reaching to secure a hairpin and she
completed the movement before she spoke, without any hint
of awkwardness. The hem of her dress was damp; he could
tell by the way it moved as she came around the desk toward
him, saying something about the weather. And he wondered
what she had been doing, out in the rain, and realized that he
would have believed anything at all. Posting a letter or riding
a white horse or dancing around a pagan altar.

As he settled into a chair he was astonished to hear himself
say, 'My wife has died.' And it terrified him, the way she had
so effortlessly drawn those words from his very heart, words
he hadn't even realized were lurking there. He wondered if
she was at all aware of this power, and many years later he
still wondered. From that moment he was always somehow on
guard with her, he couldn't help it, for she was someone who
could lay you bare in an instant. Just once, when the girls
showed him the official letter, when they quietly went about

45

gathering up the things they would need, just then did he try to speak, to enlist her help. She pretended she didn't know what he meant, pretended they were just two people, talking about two other people. He had left as quickly as he could, numbed by another loss.

And later in the shop his heart was sick, watching them try things on. The heavy rubber, the ridiculous headgear, and all he could see was the two of them, bobbing alone in the vast grey waste of some ocean.

Soldiers

Hugh told us this story, about a man named Baker. Known as
Silly Sam when he worked as a comedian, before. One day he
was blown up; they dug him out quite quickly and he seemed
to be all right. They were due to be relieved in a few days
anyway and they'd lost so many men they couldn't spare him,
so he stayed in the line. But as it happened there was a push
somewhere and their relief didn't come for nearly two weeks,
and Baker had to be sent back before that, because he started
to cry. Slowly at first, a few tears splashing onto his muddy
knees where he crouched, trying to eat a chunk of bread. The
concussion, they all thought, it does funny things to your
body. But it got worse. *This makes no sense*, Baker would say,
I'm the happiest man in France! It stopped when he was
sleeping, but they had little time for that, and the moment he
opened his eyes the tears began to well up, to roll down his
cheeks, splash on his tunic front. So thick and fast he had to
wipe his cheeks constantly, and in the end he was so busy
doing that that he couldn't even hold his rifle. Then they sent
him back.

Soldiers

II

There was a pig of a man named Smythe. Little pale eyes, flicking like a snake's. In the canteen, when the cigarettes were gone, the battered cauldrons of cocoa empty. 'Let me help you with that,' lifting the heavy pot from the fire. Then an arm about the waist, squeezing, his breath foul, stained teeth beneath the moustache and stubbly chin rubbing, and then a voice said, 'That's enough,' and he was gone, scuttering out the back door. That was how we first met Hugh.

Soldiers

III

It was only a trick of the Paris traffic that had us pause
behind them. The woman's face turned to look behind.
Nothing in her expression, just the fact that she was looking
back. It was a staff car, we could see the dark shape of the
driver's head, looking straight in front. And we thought – for
this is how we've changed or learned – well, maybe she'll get
a decent meal out of it, maybe he'll take her somewhere
where the cutlery sparkles and nothing is in short supply, the
officer belonging to the scratchy-uniformed arm that rested
on the seat behind her. And just as we thought that, his large
white hand splayed on the back of her head, forcing it down.

And we remembered Neufchateau, the Hotel Agriculture in
the afternoon. Waiting in that dingy, smoky lobby for
someone to get us out of there. Across the street a few tables
crowded the narrow sidewalk, and we went there, finally, to
drink a cup of coffee. Beside us, two soldiers and a boy of ten
or eleven. They were giving him tumblers of wine to drink,
and chocolate from their pockets. He didn't speak any
English, but they kept putting their hands on his shoulders,
saying, 'Friends, oui? Friends.'

These men are also dying in the trenches – can it be right
to think that less of a tragedy? The cowards, the liars, the
bullies, and worse. They are also fighting for their country.

Thinking about Home

Everyone did it. Talked about it. *Say, these toy trains wouldn't get you anywhere back home, would they?* Or, *They do have funny notions about breakfast here, don't they, nothing like back home.* After all, what was there to talk about here? The dead, the rain, the rotten food. Rumours, of course. Germans here and there, we were smashing them, no we weren't. It was a balance, thinking about home; it was necessary. To remind yourself, keep on reminding yourself who you were. That you had not always gone for three days without combing your hair. That there was another kind of life, that you had lived it.

No one talked much about going back after; there was a superstitious reluctance to do that. But stories, memories, most of us young enough to have school pranks fresh in our minds. It was something to hold on to, too.

Try to imagine this. A refugee train unloading at a station, the noise and the smell and the smoke swirling and rising, drawing your eyes for a moment to the cavernous dark roof, girders and blackness and malevolent foggy steam – don't want to look there, like looking into a nightmare under a child's bed. Now, say you look down again and see a young girl, nine or ten maybe, who looks around and around but seems to be alone in that crowd. She is wearing a dress that might once have been blue, might once have had a pattern, tiny white flowers maybe. You know that someone must have made her this dress, that it was a pretty thing; you know from the age of the girl that she probably loved it, tried it on and twirled around a warm kitchen. Probably there was a swing outside, and you can see her swinging on it, see her toes pointing in neat black shoes. What's on her feet now may be shoes, tied round and round with string to hold them. Her legs are streaked with mud and dried blood, as is every bit of her that you can see. She's clutching a baby in her arms, wrapped in bits of someone's coat; a green button winks for a moment as it catches a stray bit of light. What you can see of the baby's head is also bloody and muddy; it is very still, and you hope that it is sleeping.

The child scans the crowd, her head moves back and forth, her eyes flick here and there, but you can tell from those eyes that she doesn't expect to recognize anyone. So as you make your way to her, as you bend down so that she can hear you, as you bend down to take a closer look at the bundle she is carrying, which is now making tiny mewling sounds, as you, still stooping, put an arm about her narrow shoulders and feel what you couldn't see, the way her whole body trembles as if it will never stop, as you move her with her sleepwalker's stumble toward the big red cross and whatever can be done – as you do all that, you find you are remembering a doll you had once, after Ophelia, the way you took it everywhere with you, fed it and talked to it just like a real baby. And that makes you remember green grass and the feeling of sunlight on your skin, someone's voice singing, a host of things. If you couldn't do that, it's hard to know what would happen. Probably you would just die for sorrow.

It's different, of course, for those who have children at home, or obligations. Mrs Moore frets and frets about her married daughter, who is having her first baby soon. How she never liked vegetables and probably isn't watching her diet, how even a scraped knee would make her howl like the end of the world. The men show pictures and read out bits of letters they've received, all the clever and naughty things going on in a home they can walk through every time they close their eyes. Even the horrible Smythe has three little Smythes and their mother folded in his front pocket. Or for some there are worries about a business, is it being run all right, will the right decisions be made while they're away. So that even if they don't speak about *after*, it's always there, and home is something to go back to.

It's not the same for us. Once, on a hospital visit, there was a boy with no hands. He'd been reaching for something or someone when the shell came; he was not too badly hurt, except for that. But he needed someone to write letters for him, of course, and someone to hold his cigarettes. He had beautiful hair, that boy, thick and dark and very curly. It kept tumbling over his forehead and he kept trying to lift his arm, to brush it back. 'You should get someone to cut it,' we said as we smoothed it back again and again. 'Oh, my girl would never forgive me for that,' he said. 'She loves to do just what you're doing.' When we held the cigarette to his lips, he seemed to kiss our fingertips.

In another bed in that ward there was a boy who was not expected to live. He was getting huge doses of morphine, but even when he was asleep his lips would twitch. And when he was, not awake – he was never that – but semiconscious, he repeated a list of words over and over. Oak, beech, ash, elm, maple, oak beech ash elm maple. The boy with the beautiful hair said at first they thought he was just naming trees, but then someone heard *Main* and someone heard *Water* and they guessed that he was reciting the names of streets, the names of streets in whatever town he came from. His company had been hit hard; those that survived had been moved on and no one in the hospital knew yet what town it was. Some of the men in the ward thought it was a small place, that he was naming every street in the town. But most of them thought it was a route he was walking. Oak-Beech-Ash-Elm-Maple-Main-Water. The way to school, maybe, or the way to his girlfriend's house. The way to his own house from the station. Over and over he walked it, Oak-Beech-Ash-Elm-Maple-Main-Water, and after a while we could see it ourselves. See the tall trees leaning over the sidewalks, the shady verandas, the storefronts on Main Street, the cooler air on Water. If it was evening, we could smell the blossoms.

As the morphine wore off his voice got louder and louder, and after he'd had the next shot he'd sometimes stop suddenly in the middle of his list, even in the middle of a word. And someone else would finish for him: '___ple, Main, Water –' and we realized that along with everything else they were doing, or saying, or thinking, every man on that ward was walking along with him.

Our own thinking about home had that obsessive quality. Things we went over and over, trying to get the truth of. Maybe that was the difference between us and Mrs Moore, us and the men with their pockets full of photographs. Home for us was not exactly something to hold on to, it was something to figure out, to understand. So many things seemed strange, there in France. It did not seem possible that our life was as we remembered it. But we both remembered it, so wasn't that some kind of proof? We were not together every minute of our childhood, every minute of our lives, although most, perhaps. But there must have been times when one of us was in a room but not the other. When only one of us saw something, heard something, was spoken to. But we don't remember anything like that. This is something you have to understand, if you are to understand anything. The things we talked about in the wet tent, in the wooden room at Chalons – we shared them all. And if there was a split second, the tiniest of moments, briefer than the blink of an eye, when one of us said something – then in that briefest of moments the other had the memory, could hear, feel, taste it.

Interview

The journalist was fresh from home, and his questions made
us realize how far away that was. The last thing he asked was
for one thing, one experience, that would give his readers –
the folks, he called them – an idea of what it was really like.
So we told him about travelling a road near Ancerville, where
the bombardment had been heavy a few days before. How we
stopped to stretch our legs for a moment. And found a small,
perfect child's hand, lying palm up in the dust.

Nan

I don't see so well now; perhaps that's why the memory
pictures are so clear. Know what I mean by memory pictures?
Of course you do; everybody's got them. I've been thinking
about it ever since I heard. Seeing it clear as day. The path
that led off the kitchen garden and down to the river. The two
of them running ahead of me, trees overhanging and sunlight
falling through and their feet kicking up behind them. And I
thought *Run, girls, keep running. Run right out of this.* So
maybe I always knew.

I was going to leave service long ago; that was my plan. My
sister had a cottage in a little place by the sea, and I was
going to go and live there with her. Before I got too old to
walk along the sand, to really live there. We grew up on an
island, you see, and I always missed it. That clean wind
blowing, the smell of it. So I was going to see her through the
birthing, stay just until they got someone else settled in. I
owed them that; they'd been so generous to me. Not *owed*
exactly, but anyway that's what I agreed to. I'd been with
Miss Alice since she was a girl, and when she asked me I
couldn't say no. But one thing I've learned is that this life
always has surprises in store, and most of them aren't the
kind to make you jump for joy. It was the two of them that
did her in. She'd never been strong, Miss Alice, but she was so
lively. It was a happy house, before. Break your heart to see it
happen. So of course I couldn't just walk away. Stayed until
the girls were grown, did my best. My sister died and I never
did get to that cottage by the sea, but it's not so bad here. It
took her so long to die, poor soul, but it was written on her
face from before the birth. Things changed overnight, it
seemed, like the heart went out of that house, leaving nothing
but a lot of echoing rooms. Even the boys changed, became
sly and sad. I had to keep a sharp eye when the girls were

small, even though I couldn't believe they would really harm them. There was that business with the fountain – we never did get to the truth of that. Everyone so busy blaming that useless Susan for falling asleep.

What were they like as children? Like children, of course. They learned to walk and talk, they had tea parties for their dolls and played on the lawns. Perhaps more serious than most but that's not surprising, the house being the way it was and the Mister never what you could call a warm man. I used to fancy I could tell them apart, though if you asked me I couldn't say how. Alike as two peas in a pod they were, and if one had a stomachache the other would too, without fail. When they were small, four or five maybe, they had a special language they spoke to each other. A lot of made-up words that they seemed to understand. *Brimble* meant cake; I remember I figured that out, but for the rest I had no idea. It used to make me a little cross, if I tell the truth, the way they would sit whispering nonsense together as if no one else mattered at all. But there, they only had each other all those years. I thought it would be good for them when they went off to Miss Reilly's school, thought they would somehow open, make lots of new friends. They did bring girls home once in a while, but not often. Still, they were good girls, never a moment's trouble. Except for the way they used to go to the river; many's the time I've scolded them for that. And the day of Miss Alice's funeral, poor little mites. They adored that Miss Reilly; she has a lot to answer for, in my opinion. Always going on about the state of the world, about hunger and injustice. 'Miss Reilly says women can change the world,' they told me more than once. Now I don't deny this world needs some changing, but why should it be my poor girls to do it? I used to be delighted when they'd accept an invitation to a dance or a party. I'd wait up for them with a pot of cocoa and we'd sit around the kitchen table like we used to when they were small. 'Thank heavens that's over,' they always said.

56

'The silliness, Nan, you just wouldn't believe.' Talking to them was like talking to one person, always was, the way they started and finished each other's sentences. I used to wonder how they would ever get married and have a normal life; it was impossible to imagine them separated like that.

They came to see me before they went away. I'd left the house of course, but they still came to visit me often, always brought some of that shortbread I like. They were wearing their uniforms, and very smart they looked. Sort of a greenish whipcord with blue ties and little blue hats with the brims curved down. They said there were also heavy long capes, so I didn't have to worry about them being cold. They didn't stay long; their eyes were bright as they told me about all the things they still had to gather up. I could see it was no use but I tried anyway, told them there was plenty of war work right here at home. Told them to think of their father, with James gone and only Marcus for company. They'd thought of all that, well, of course they had. But they were convinced that they were meant to do their bit overseas. When they left I watched them from my window, as they walked away side by side down the street. I felt it in my bones, and it turns out I was right; I knew I'd never see them again.

In the Cellar

We met Elizabeth in the cellar of the Hotel Terminus, during an *alerte*. It was not so crowded that night. Two small children curled against their mother, so tired that only the loudest bangs made them flinch. An old woman with a maid and an ugly little dog. Several others who were just huddled shapes under blankets – the staff, perhaps, who often slept in the cellar to avoid having their sleep interrupted by the journey, night after night.

It was surprising that we recognized Elizabeth, for she was very changed. But we were too, so perhaps that gave us eyes to recognize each other. She was fully dressed; she said that she'd been in Paris a week, waiting to be moved out again, that she'd spent so many nights shivering in her dressing gown that she'd finally decided to just sleep in her clothes. We talked for a long time, speaking softly, for the children's mother had finally fallen asleep too. There was something about their pale faces, the way they breathed in unison, that broke your heart, there in the cellar.

Elizabeth was terribly thin; she said she'd had the flu, although she was much better. She said that in her last hospital there'd been a nurse who'd come across on a ship struck by flu. Like the worst nightmare, Elizabeth said. Like a ghost ship, people dead all over it, scores of them, and barely enough left standing to sail the ship. And then we talked of our own crossing, of the time the handsome officer asked Elizabeth to dance and she vomited all down the front of his uniform, how she thought she'd die of shame. 'Strange, isn't it,' she said, 'the things that mattered then.' And we knew what she meant.

We were afraid to ask about Art, but then she told us that her mother had received word the very day we all arrived in France. Now she was trying to find the place where he was buried. 'I have to do that, at least,' Elizabeth said. 'I can't go home and face them unless I've done that.' She'd even bought a little camera, so she could take pictures of the spot when she found it.

'I don't know how I can go home anyway,' Elizabeth said. 'Do you? How can we do it, how can we go back to our own table, our own beds, as if we were the same people? I feel broken,' she said, in the flickering candlelight in the cellar of the Hotel Terminus. 'Something is broken in me. It's all just a horrible mess, and there's no meaning in any of it.'

Was it right or wrong, what we did then? Holding Elizabeth's hands and telling her it was all worthwhile. That it did have meaning, that we were right to be where we were, doing what we were doing. That the world would be different, after. A better place. Was it right or wrong, at that moment, to tell Elizabeth things we no longer believed?

When the bugle sounded we made our way back up to our rooms; there was still enough of the night left to make sleep possible, if there wasn't another *alerte*. We arranged to meet for breakfast the next day, but in the morning Elizabeth was gone and we didn't see her again.

The Sea King

We know, of course we know, that it's just a story Nan told.
Spun out of her Irish dreams and taking hold in ours. Those
nights of soft rain a long time ago, in a sloping room at the
top of the fragile house. But we live in a world where everything
we know has been proved wrong, a world gone completely
mad. If this world can exist, then anything is possible.

Nan said the Sea King lived at the deepest bottom, where
only the drowned men go. He had power over the oceans and
the rivers, and all things that moved upon them. And the
schools of swimming fish were his spies and messengers,
bringing back news from the farthest reaches of his kingdom.
He was fierce and angry and the gates of his palace were built
from dead men's bones. A mound of skulls guarded his
treasure room, chests filled with gold and jewels from ships he
had caused to sink. Sometimes a chest broke open as it
spiralled slowly down to the depths, and the sea floor for
miles around the palace was littered with precious stones that
glowed in the greenish light. The Sea King's children played
games with those gems, and arranged them in intricate patterns
that could sometimes be glimpsed if you looked down through
clear water on a still, sunny day. There were also beautiful
necklaces that had lain around the necks of drowned women,
and they floated gently down to that quiet place.

In Nan's stories the Sea King brought nothing but storms
and death, his rage against the world. But in a world gone
mad, a world where everything had been proved wrong, we
wondered if that was too. Perhaps his kingdom was a
beautiful, gentle place, his wrath really sorrow, pining for lost
children who had disappeared into the world of men. Perhaps
that's who we are, perhaps we really are the Sea King's
beautiful daughters. Lost, long lost, wandering ill at ease
through the world of foggy air.

Classmates

We ran into them in Paris, the way you ran into people you knew in the war. Sitting at a table outside the Café de la Paix, across from the Opéra. Weren't we surprised to see them there, with their hair cut short, just like ours. Though when I think of it, back home they used to help out in soup kitchens and raise money for things, so perhaps it was not so strange that they came to the war. They only had three nights in Paris and they'd already spent two down in the Gare du Nord, helping with refugee trains and feeding soldiers. We went on to Rumpelmayer's for tea and ice cream – very watery, as usual – and then they came back to the Hive for the evening. Marjorie played her funny little piano a bit, and Jess and Molly from across the hall popped in and we had a grand old time, talking about old friends. It was quite astonishing how many had turned up in Paris at one time or another.

They were the same as always, maybe a little more so. Quiet, I mean. How I envied them, being up close to the front. Marjorie and I worked at the refugee centre, and it's not that that wasn't important. Finding clothes for the poor things and a place to stay, whatever bits of furniture we could lay our hands on. Scrambling always to find *essence* for the old car we drove around in. But somehow it didn't feel like really being in the war – I don't know why. It certainly looked like it – soldiers everywhere and all the statues sandbagged, shop windows taped. The dark streets at night, only an occasional dim blue light. No hot water except on Saturday, no coffee, no meat most days. But all the restaurants and cafés were open, shows at night, people filling the streets – it was all such *fun*. Even when the big gun boomed, you would see people flinch, then shrug and carry on, maybe checking their watch to see how long before the next shell. We were all mad to go to the front, just to see it, and we hoped to arrange an excursion. I remember how they looked when we said that. It reminded me of the old school days, how they always seemed a little too good for the world. Not snobbish, I don't mean that at all. But you know how when you get a couple of hundred girls together there are always rivalries and tiffs and dramas. Well they were never drawn into any of that; I don't remember a single time. They always kept themselves apart; they always seemed to have a certain standard of behaviour. I've often thought that this world must have been a constant disappointment to them.

Yellow Leaves

We weren't expecting the noise. Could have had no idea how it would be. Not the guns and explosions when we were near the front; that's a particular agony. And even far away, an undertone. But more the constant ruckus, living in a large group of people. The shouting in the camp, the singing and sounds of hammering. Horses and motors and airplanes if they're near. The racket in the canteen or mess hall, always something. There's no place for contemplation, no space for it, every waking moment, and even sleeping ones, filled up with sound.

On our last morning at home we woke early and went to sit in the silence on the kitchen porch. A cold morning, the grass rimed with frost that was just beginning to glisten as the sun touched it. The distant line of silent, coloured hills. We didn't speak, just tried to take it in, our stomachs in nagging, queasy knots, which eased a little as the sun reached the spot where we sat. It was completely still, no sound from the sleeping house behind us, no bird or animal.

But then there *was* a sound. We gradually became aware of it, a wrenching, tearing, rattling sound, becoming louder and more constant as we listened to it. It sounded like – something, and yet like nothing we'd ever heard before. And then we saw a flicker of movement, and understood what was happening. As the sun warmed the frosted yellow maples that ringed the back garden the leaves began to detach with a snap, fall with an icy clatter. First one, then another, then more and more, a shower. On our last morning we realized that we had been living in a silence so absolute that we could hear the sound each leaf makes as it falls.

It can never be like that again. This is the sound of the modern world, the world we are fighting for. The tramp tramp tramp of a thousand feet marching, the jingle of

harnesses and medals. The shriek of train whistles, the rattle
of a clean gun being assembled, the howls of men in pain.

Letter

Dear Anne,

Thank you for your last letter, and all the news of home. It's good to be reminded; we feel so far away in this new life we are living. As you see, the black pen is working beautifully – it's a pity the paper doesn't do it justice.

We were glad to hear that Father was well when last you saw him. He writes that the business is booming, and to tell you the truth we are dismayed that someone so close to us is growing rich out of all this suffering. Father would say that's the way of the world, but surely that's what we are fighting to change.

We are just back from a few days' leave in Paris – you wouldn't recognize the place. Soldiers and sandbags everywhere, shop windows taped up. Taxis charge exorbitant rates after dark, and it's very difficult to find your way at night, with only the blue lights marking the shelters. But the cafés and restaurants are full, and life goes on, even though every second person you see is dressed in mourning. We met up with Jane and Marjorie and spent a pleasant evening in their apartment, which they call the Hive because they've painted everything yellow and black. They are working very hard at one of the refugee centres, but still having a grand time – you remember they were such jolly girls. It must be very gratifying to know that so many of your old girls are here, doing their bit with the same spirit that carried us through all those marches and rallies. Let anyone who still doubts women's capabilities just see what we are doing, over here and at home, in this time of crisis.

We sometimes wonder if we could better serve helping with the refugees, who number in the thousands, pitiful souls, often with nothing more than the clothes on their backs. Or in a hospital – the work the nurses and doctors are doing is nothing short of heroic. We constantly feel that there should be more we can do. But we know that our work is important too. It was explained to us on our first day that we are here to provide a civilizing influence in the camp, an alternative to the filthy *estaminets* and the women who appear wherever soldiers are gathered. And the men appreciate what we do for them. We get to know some; they tell us about their lives back home, and we wonder what happens to them when they leave. It is horrible to think that many will have been wounded or killed. The front is moving closer; we often hear the guns and think of the men out there fighting. The camp is on standby, ready to move at a moment's notice, and this is very hard on the nerves.

We have just received word that there is to be a dance tonight; of all our duties this is the most onerous. The dances are held every few weeks in a nearby camp, and though canteen workers and sometimes nurses are brought in from miles around there are never enough women for the hundreds of men who come to them. The room is bright and rather hot and smelly from all the bodies packed in. Usually there's a Victrola, or sometimes a real band. A whistle blows every two minutes to change partners, and sometimes there are terrible fights. All for two minutes' shuffle around the floor with a woman in your arms. For that's what we are at these times, Women, and not ourselves at all. It is a most disheartening experience, and no matter how many times we are assured that it is important for morale we can't help thinking, as we pull our aching heads and feet into the truck for the ride home, that it's not at all what we came to France for.

Two weeks ago we saw our first Germans, wounded prisoners in the hospital where we help out on our free day. And the strange thing was they were just like our boys, frightened and in pain. So young. They were so excited that we spoke some German, for they speak no English and only one knows a little French. We helped one write a letter to his mother – heaven knows if she'll ever receive it – and you know, it was so much like the letters we write for our boys, full of the same concerns and reassurances. Many of the men say that they hate the generals who run the war far more than the 'enemy'. Oh, sometimes this war seems like a terrible machine, carried along by its own momentum. Chewing up lives and spitting them out. We do our work day by day and try not to think about the enormity of it. The destruction, the horror, the waste. And it seems like it will go on and on, until there are no young men left in the world. We wonder then if we did the right thing by coming here, by being part of it.

Sainte Germaine

In Bar-sur-Aube we asked Hugh what it was like.

'Boring,' he said. 'If it wasn't for the terror, we'd all
be bored to death. It's hard to explain. Like a dream,
it's something like a dream. I don't mean like a nightmare,
not just that. But things have their own logic, things operate
by their own rules, and it makes some kind of sense,
at the front, although it would make none at all in the real
world.'

We were sitting at a little table, on a narrow white-walled
street. Hugh had persuaded us that we needed an outing on
our free day, that we needed to get right away from the war.
He said he would organize everything. We had stopped
asking, or even wondering, how Hugh was always able to lay
his hands on things. Old cars or bicycles or new bars of soap.
Something very close to real coffee, day passes. He just
seemed to manage, that's how it was with him.

The little street was just off the shady town square, where
three or four women chatted by the ancient well; now and
then they would shake their heads, hand on cheek.

'This should be what's real,' Hugh said. 'What's been
forever, what will go on, long after we're gone.'

Another woman had come to the well, was drawing up
water, and we knew he was thinking of the deep grooves we'd
noticed in the grey stone, how many hundreds of years it had
taken bucket ropes to make them. But what we also noticed
was the way the chatting group seemed to register the other's
presence, without pausing in their conversation or turning
their heads. To our eyes, she looked like one of them. About
the same age, dressed in much the same way. Nothing, to our
eyes, that would explain why the little group turned away
from her, without actually moving. The way she seemed
oblivious, yet the set of her back, walking away, showed she

was not. And we thought how Hugh's words meant this as well.

We went a few miles out of the town to swim, to a place where the river eddied in a deep green pool. We changed in the trees, thankful for that frivolous impulse, long ago and far away, that made us squeeze our swimming costumes into our bulging trunks. When we emerged from the trees Hugh said, 'Good God, even the scars match,' and we looked down at our pale legs, the paler web of lines. We might have shown him then how the scars didn't quite match, but he turned away quickly, embarrassed, we supposed, to be looking.

It was one of the things we liked about Hugh, the way he didn't ever play that tedious game of trying to tell us apart. Most people did, and had done all our lives. As if together we were too much for them, as if the only way they could deal with us was to divide, to diminish us. But Hugh had always accepted us just as we were, just as we were with each other.

Soldiers loved to play the guessing game. Our first day at the canteen, Mrs Moore gave us a little talk. 'Girls,' she said, 'you must always remember that these boys don't expect to see their old age, and many of them won't. So we have to make some – allowances. Of course I don't mean that anyone has to put up with any real unpleasantness. But we must try not to be shocked if their behaviour, their conversation, is not always what we would demand in our own parlours.'

Dear Mrs Moore, with her friend Dr Thomas, who came discreetly calling, and Colonel McAndrew not so long after the doctor was sent home. But we remembered her words, we consciously made allowances those first weeks, before we grew our skin. But one night there was a mood in the canteen. An edge to the laughter, to the tone of the voices. Most of the men were going up to the line the next day and drifted away early, but twenty or thirty lingered, playing our two records over and over. A few of them were standing about near our

69

counter, and one of them came over and said, 'My friends don't believe I can tell you apart, will you help me out?'

And we said all right, and smiled when we said it, thinking of Mrs Moore and thinking that though we were heartily sick of this game, it was little enough to do for this poor boy, on what might well be his last evening on earth. He had a mess of short reddish hair, that boy, and very pale eyelashes. One eye seemed noticeably smaller than the other, with a dark brown mole on his cheek beneath it. He didn't look old enough to shave, but there was a pale, reddish stubble on his chin.

His friends drew closer as he gave us directions. 'Turn away from me, right round. Now turn back, look at me. Smile. Frown. Reach up, pretend you're taking pins from your hair. Touch your cheeks together, yes, that's good. Stay like that. Now touch each other's cheeks, but slowly, very slowly.'

His tongue came out to lick his bottom lip. The record needle had come to the end of the long, long trail and hissed and scratched, and that seemed to be the only sound. 'Now,' he said, and we wondered why we had thought him a boy when the look in his mismatched eyes was ancient. 'Now –' And we said, 'Time's up,' and turned away, busying ourselves with things behind the counter, laughing as if it had all been harmless.

Willows grew on the farther bank and dappled the light on the surface of the river. It was marvellous to be swimming, and we laughed and splashed and ducked each other and Hugh swam beneath us and tickled the soles of our feet. And we stayed in the water after he climbed out, and he watched us, lying on the grassy bank, smoking a cigarette and looking completely contented. We floated on our backs, on our stomachs, arms and legs splayed, and dived down to see if we could reach the bottom. And there was something magical in that pale green underwater light, in the fronded weeds that waved and beckoned us down. It was deeper than we thought; our hair floated free behind us, and we reached out a hand to each other, fingertips skimmed, and missed.

And there was, suddenly, a moment of cold panic. Cold, as if the water itself had chilled and darkened, inexplicable. We kicked to the surface, flailed our way to the bank where Hugh lounged, felt the sun begin to warm us again, our racing hearts slow down. We didn't speak of it.

'So, kids,' Hugh said, squinting against the smoke rising from his cigarette, 'how did you get those scars?' And we surprised ourselves by telling him. It was one of those things we didn't talk about, except to each other. From a time we didn't talk about, either, except to each other. The summer our mother died, the day our brothers were allowed to go to the party, and we were not. We prowled the garden in a rage, hitting at things with sticks and stones, and shattered a pane of glass that guarded the tomatoes and then shattered more, the sound become intoxicating. And some time later we sat on the grass facing each other, toe to toe, and drew on our skin with a shard of that glass, copying the moves exactly. Blood rolling down to pool in our folded stockings. Oh what a fuss when Nan found us. It hurt then, and later, but the wounds healed quickly, leaving identical scars. Identical but reversed, of course, from sitting toe to toe.

'What's it like?' Hugh asked later. It was so peaceful there in the sunlight. The only sound the wind through the trees, a bell far away.

'It's safe,' we said. 'No matter what happens you're not alone,' we said.

'Isn't that supposed to be God?' he said.

And then Hugh said that of everyone over here he maybe felt sorriest for the chaplains, and then he told us about the old aunt who'd raised him, the widow of his father's brother, and how he had scars himself, from the whippings. She used a switch, willow maybe, and they had to pray on their knees before and after. But he said he never could hold it against her. Because after a whipping she'd go to her room and he'd hear her. Muffled, like her face was in a pillow, which it probably was. Sobbing as if her heart would break.

'She wasn't a cruel woman,' Hugh said. 'She was doing what she truly believed had to be done. And it tormented her.'

We asked about his parents, but he said he didn't know much about them, had never even seen a picture. His aunt told him they had just died, but he never quite believed her. He threw himself back, hands beneath his head, and spoke to the sky, to the overhanging trees.

'I was five or six when I came to her, and I don't remember anything at all before that. Strange, isn't it? Five or six years is a long time, you'd think there'd be something. Their faces, looking at me, the sound of their voices.'

Once he heard his aunt telling a woman from the church that he'd lived just like a gypsy, and he got the idea that his parents really were gypsies, that they'd somehow misplaced him and that one day they'd look around and realize he was missing, come back for him. And they'd all drive away together in a brightly painted caravan, pulled by a horse named Old Joe.

'And every morning, early, I'd hear the milkman's horse and think – well, you know,' Hugh said. 'Her husband was a parson, and after he died she must have thought that her life would go a certain way. But she took me in, and so it went another way. What was that like for her? She knew nothing about children, she had no – imagination. And I was a handful, no question. I fought her all the way. It wasn't easy.'

The wind moved through the trees, and when Hugh spoke again, it was in a posh voice. 'Time we were going,' he said. 'We have reservations at a charming little inn nearby.'

When he sat up we saw the marks on his back and without
thinking we reached out to touch them. His skin shuddered
beneath our fingers, and we snatched them back. And asked
how he could be so understanding.

'Oh, there was my friend Tom,' he said. 'I met him very
soon after I came there, in this dusty little laneway behind our
houses. He laughed at the clothes she'd put me in, but then he
said I could share his parents, as I didn't have my own. That's
the kind of fellow Tom was, even then. And I suppose I did
share his family, in a way. Certainly his house always felt
more like home to me. They were a grand bunch – well, they
still are, of course. So much laughter. So I was lucky, you see.
I always had that to balance things, to show me there was
another way. Otherwise – well, who knows?'

Hugh really did know of an inn nearby; we sat outside on the
edge of a great cliff with the fan-shaped Aube valley spread
out below us. The small square fields in shades of green and
yellow and the white road snaking north. And there were
omelettes and sausages, salad, and it all tasted wonderful, in
a way you could only understand if you'd spent time picking
lumps of gristle from a mess tin. We all grew a little giddy on
the local wine and looked down the valley as the light began
to fade.

Hugh said the place was the cliff of Sainte Germaine, and
he told us the story, though not how he'd learned it. How long
ago the conqueror Attila was camped on top of the cliff, right
where we were now giggling and eating. And he sent word
down to the town of Bar to send their prettiest girl up to him,
or he would destroy them all. So a beautiful girl named
Germaine came up the steep path, slowly and steadily, but
when she reached the top, before anyone could stop her or
even guess what was in her mind, she broke and ran, threw
herself over the cliff to the valley far below.

It was easy to imagine it in that place, as the light began to fade and ancient shadows appeared. The girl climbing through them, her breath coming a little harder as she went. Hearing the sound of the camp as she came nearer, probably not so different from the sounds of a modern army camp at rest. Knowing that this was happening to her simply because she was a girl, because she was pleasing to look at, which should not have been a bad thing. The flames of the torches, as she drew nearer, the bellowing of animals. The escape.

We talked then about whether it took more courage to live or to die, in such a situation. And argued a little; Hugh said one should always choose life, that was the only way for the human spirit to triumph.

'Otherwise,' he said. 'The bravest and the best are dying every day. Otherwise there'll only be scoundrels like me left to run the world.'

As we stood to go, we asked Hugh if there was some kind of stone or marker at the place where Sainte Germaine leapt.

'No idea,' he said. 'Maybe I made it all up.'

And we chased him all the way back to the motor.

On the drive we slept; it was completely dark. I woke once and the two of them were laughing at something I hadn't heard.

Hugh

And what did Hugh want? It should have been a simple
thing. He wanted a quiet place, that was all. A place where he
didn't have to do anything, be anything, a place where he
could just lay his head down. He wanted to be close to
something soft and human.

He thought of Tom's older sisters sometimes, the way he
ran in and out of their lives all his childhood, the way they
always made a space for him. Stopped whatever they were
doing to smile, to say 'Hello, Hugh,' sometimes a big hug
when he was smaller. The wonder of what they had to give
him.

There was a girl back home who tried. Wrote letters about
missing him, asked questions he couldn't possibly answer. She
wanted to know what it was like, she wanted to be able to
imagine him, day by day. How could he tell her anything at
all? It wasn't the thought of the censors that stopped him, it
was the fact that she would have to be there to even begin to
imagine it, and even then she couldn't have believed it. He
couldn't believe it himself. He knew there must have been
stages; it didn't all happen at once. He and Tom sitting in
their secret place on the riverbank, the cave they'd made
when they were boys, from shrubs and low hanging branches.
There was still a rotting bit of mat on the ground, and he
remembered how at one time they'd rolled it up and hidden it
in a hole they'd dug beneath an old log, how they carefully
wiped out their footprints with a fanned branch kept for that
purpose. They went there, alone or together, all through their
childhood, eating sweet things filched from Tom's house,
making fishing poles and lures, carving bits of wood with the
knives they were not allowed to have. It filled him with
wonder, always, that people could pass by and not notice the
little notch in the tree trunk, that they would assume, if they

thought about it at all, that the log had fallen just so, that the fanned branch was just like any other. That, if you didn't know what to expect, you would never think to look for it.

The afternoon he and Tom decided to join up they sat outside the cave drinking bottles of beer, too big now to be comfortable hunched inside. They accused each other of leaving the mat out, the mat he had taken from his aunt's spare room and never even been questioned about, for she could never imagine he would want such a thing. It had been years since either one had been there; neither would admit to being the last. Hugh wondered sometimes if other boys had found the place, would wonder themselves about that bit of cloth and who had brought it there. But he knew it was already earth-coloured, already rotted to nothing.

And he knew that there must have been stages, between that afternoon and this. The crisp autumn sky above them, the sound of the river, so close yet only glimpsed from where they sat. He couldn't have gone straight from that to this, become this creature in the line who was just so incredibly weary. The rank smell of himself that he no longer noticed, but assumed. The thick taste in his mouth, the itching and grime all over his body, his hands thickened and scarred, fingernails blackened from bangs and injuries he hadn't even noticed. The girl at home knitted him warm stockings and thick pullovers the colour of smoke. He wiggled and yanked the boots from his foul, soupy feet, peeled or sometimes cut off the old socks and pulled on the new. He thought of her fleetingly then, thought that whatever she imagined, stitch by stitch in the lamp glow, it could never be this, could never come close to this.

All he wanted was something simple, and he thought for a while he'd found it. The first night in camp he went to the canteen, not wanting, suddenly, to spend another evening in an *estaminet*, with rough wine and bragging soldiers' talk. The canteen was crowded, thick with smoke and mugs of cocoa, a record playing, gingham curtains at the windows. He found himself a corner with a pile of old magazines and tried to settle himself to read, but there was a restlessness in him, a twitching, and he thought maybe a glass of wine after all. And then he saw them behind the counter, just standing side by side, and in the same instant they each raised an arm, brushed the hair from their foreheads with the back of a hand, and something in that paired gesture brought a great peace to settle on him, as if it were something he'd been waiting to see all his life.

When the canteen closed a couple of men stayed behind to help tidy up and he stayed too, and when all the chairs were straightened, the dirty mugs collected, they all sat around in the little kitchen area, perched on chairs and crates, talking about nothing in particular. He lay down to sleep that night feeling cleaner than he had in years. And that became the pattern of his evenings. The camp was in a little dip surrounded by low hills, and after supper he would walk a particular path, sit down on a particular rock, smoke a cigarette and watch the light fade from the untouched hills. Sometimes he could hear the guns faintly, but that only made it more peaceful. Then back down to the canteen and always, after the men drifted away, the three of them left talking.

When he went back up to the line they were in a quiet sector, only firing over the top once in a while to remind themselves there was a war on, and he thought, for his aunt must have had some influence, that it was because he'd been living so purely. He thought that if he'd seen one woman raise a hand to her forehead it would have been the same old story, but it was all different because they were two. He found he even looked around in a different way, storing up things to tell them about the next time he went back. He loved to make them laugh, but he also loved the melancholy that was part of their containment, part of the seriousness that made him feel that when they spoke together they were really talking, not

77

just exchanging words. He told them things about himself that he might have told other people, but in a different way entirely, and he thought it was the same for them. When the Armistice came he was far away, and then he was sent to Germany, and that was where he saw the old newspaper. And he wasn't exactly surprised, but it still broke his heart.

About the Sentry

He was never quite the same. Not that it changed his life, not that it made him crazy or restless or morose. Or not any more than he already was. But of all the things he'd seen – and he'd seen enough to give the whole world nightmares – it was the thing that stayed with him. Not the thing that he talked about over a jug or, more rarely, lying in the dark with his wife, but the thing that stayed with him. The thing that he couldn't shake, the thing that was on his mind when his eyes snapped open, heart pounding. One minute he was hiding a smoke in his cupped hand, stamping his feet as he walked and thinking only that he was cold, that he'd be glad to get down below to the steamy light. And then nothing was ever the same again.

He blamed himself. He'd seen it time and again, some fellow with days or hours to go who let his breath out a little, started to think he'd made it. Let himself think about a chair by the fire, soft hands, loved faces. And then *wham*, and home all right, but in a shape no one would recognize. So he blamed himself, but who could have known that it would come like that, the thing that would do for him? Not that it changed his life. But how could he know? When he first saw the woman who would be his wife she was wearing a long dark dress that billowed in a cold wind.

He never talked about it, though there were times when he was close. And he thought the worst part was the way they looked right past him. Changed his life and never even noticed he was there.

Near the Field of Crosses

We all have those pictures in our heads. Those moments of memory caught and held, for some reason, and perhaps if we could string them all together they would make some sense of our lives. Not for anyone else, but for ourselves, for of course the moments we hold would not have been remembered by anyone else, on their way to their own collection. Little things. The way the light fell on a certain wall, the dappled shadow dancing there. Drops of dew glistening on a blowzy orange flower. The way the wind shifts before a storm, exposing the pale undersides of leaves, the way the lamplight strikes a particular face or the intense, wonderful melancholy of certain notes on a piano. Each cross in this field marks a nest of memories like that along with whatever is left of the person who enclosed it. And no one could ever guess, not even the closest person, just what those moments would be. Should that be chilling, or liberating?

Once, you see, I would have known that ours were shared. How can you imagine what this sudden uncertainty is like? There is a memory that I know is mine alone. Waking suddenly in a dark car, and she and Hugh were laughing, together.

In the Evening

I went to meet Hugh. Such a simple thing to say, five little
words. But oh, the chasm that opened up. I went to meet
Hugh and nothing was ever the same. I can't even say why I
went, what I expected. Only that it seemed a way to end the
turmoil. When we drove back from the place of Sainte
Germaine it was very dark, and Hugh had to drive slowly and
carefully. Ruth fell asleep in the back, and maybe it was the
wine, I don't know, I don't have much experience of wine. We
were talking, Hugh and I, in a little dark bubble moving
through a dark sea of night, and suddenly I felt such a great
opening up. And I realized, I think right then I realized, that
it was because Hugh was talking to *me*. I don't think I can
explain what that was like.

   I knew the way he walked, each evening after supper; I
had watched him. I waited until Ruth uncapped her pen,
straightened the notepaper on the writing board, and then I
said, 'I think I'll go for a bit of a stroll.' She raised her eyes,
faintly puzzled; perhaps my voice sounded as strange as it did
to my own ears. And then I was outside and then I was
walking the path that led up, out of the camp, and my
thoughts wheeled like a flock of startled birds. I settled myself
to wait by the big rock that splits the path in two, and I
waited and waited, but he didn't come.

   It was nearly dark when I came down, the canteen already
bustling. 'Sorry, I lost track of time,' I said, and the lie lay
between us, an ugly thing. Hugh didn't appear that night, but
we saw him with his kit the next morning. His eyes were red
and there was a big discoloured swelling high on one cheek.
'Knew I shouldn't have gone to Papa George's,' he said. And then
with a wave of his hand he was gone, falling in with a line of
marching men, marching down the rutted road and out of our
lives. Leaving me with a broken thing to try to put together.

Armistice

And then suddenly it was all over. A cold, misty day like so many others, breaking up packing cases to feed the fire. All morning the guns roared without pause; eleven o'clock came and went and we thought it had just been another rumour. But then gradually, so gradually, they stopped, and then there was silence. Berthe paused in her stirring and said, 'C'est fini?' Then she sank to the ground with her apron covering her eyes and huge sobs shaking her shoulders.

Later we bounced into town in a truck filled with laughing soldiers, riding up front with Corporal Easton. Every so often he would bang the steering wheel with the heel of his hand, give his shoulders a twitch and say, 'It's over, it's really over.'

The main square was still thronged with people, some crying, some dancing. There were uniforms everywhere, and women in black, and children darting through the crowd playing tag. All the windows around the square were open, and in each open window was a row of lighted candles. We had thought to treat ourselves to a meal, but every café was filled with drunken soldiers, singing and crashing glasses and bottles. A group had commandeered the town's only taxi and was screeching through the narrow streets, whooping and firing revolvers in the air. Others staggered by, their arms around local girls or around each other. It was not a place for us, and we finally managed to find a ride back to camp. We thought at least we would sleep, really sleep, but our dreams were filled with dead men.

Teacup

When our papers came we didn't know what to think. Now it
was over, really over. We were no longer necessary, we were
about to be spun loose. Into what, we wondered, and couldn't
imagine. Since the Armistice we had been moved from camp
to camp as they closed down, and that was part of the
strangeness. We missed Berthe's humming, little Albert's grin
as he dumped a stack of kindling on the kitchen floor. The
faces of men we'd come to know. The work was the same, the
big kettles of cocoa, of coffee, the piles of cigarettes and
chocolate bars. But the mood was different, the men restless
and eager to be gone. They chafed at the regulations they
were still forced to live by, cursed the drilling that filled up
their days. There were always fights. Men who had fought
side by side now ploughed their fists into each other at the
slightest excuse. Was this the new world?

And between us there was a strangeness, and that was the
worst part. Since I went to meet Hugh, since I lied. Once Mrs
Moore got a letter saying that her father had suffered a
stroke, and Dr Thomas explained it over lunch. He said it was
like a severing in the brain, and that was what this felt like.
An emptiness and a terrible thrumming panic. We were no
longer whole; we couldn't imagine how we would ever be
whole again. We thought of Nan's favourite teacup, the one
with the little blue flowers around the rim. She dropped it
once and it split in two, and she spent an evening with a pot
of glue and a matchstick, putting it back together. She still
used it after – it still held tea – but you could always see the
join.

Journey

The little train stood in the station, the few freight cars still bearing the legend *40 hommes 8 chevaux*. The platform was crowded – soldiers with their heavy packs, people with bags and bundles. And perhaps we felt it as we put our foot on the step, pulled a little with tired arms, but everyone was laughing and waving and pushing and there was no time to say *Stop. Wait.* No way to turn back against the bodies behind, to say *No, we won't go*. Pushed into our seat. The final click of the doors, our shoulders bumping hard, and the knowledge dawning with our exhaled breath that we were caught up in another thing, by another thing. The signs were still posted in the carriage. *Taisez-vous, méfiez-vous, les oreilles ennemies vous écoutent.* We spoke in whispers, if we spoke at all.

So hot on the train, no air. Crammed together, the smells rising from all those bodies, wet wool and worse, much worse. Impossible to open a window, impossible even to see through a window while the rain slashed down. Cold, hard rain. There was a time in our life when it was wonderful to sit in a window seat and watch the rain. Books in our laps, the feel of paper at our fingertips and raising our eyes again and again to look through to the dripping trees, the garden. It was possible then to imagine any hero appearing, water dripping from his cape, his wide-brimmed hat, as he looked up at our white shapes in the window. It was possible then to spend an entire day with the fire hissing, the gentle rain falling, the grey light slowly deepening. Dreaming. On the train we understood that there were no heroes, that that life could not possibly be ours.

The journey took two days. The train crawled slowly, sometimes reversing for miles, sometimes sitting motionless for an hour or more. We passed through villages blasted to piles of rubble, we passed the burnt-out shells of trucks, the splintered remains of horse-drawn carts. The roads we could see were filled with lines of people, walking with heads down, shoulders hunched against the rain. They had the look of people who had been walking forever, who would never reach their destination.

There was a soldier sitting beside us; he named the battlefields we passed near. His foot was bandaged, crutches leaning against the seat.

'I hurt it playing football yesterday,' he said. 'My only war wound, can you believe it?'

He showed us photographs of his girlfriend, of his parents and younger brother. We saw our own hands reaching out to take them, heard our own voices, but all the time there was a terrible pounding in our heads.

Towards evening of the first day the rain stopped and the train moved into the night. And it was like that, moving *into* night, as if it were a strange new country. We had dinner tickets but we let them fall to the muddy floor, the bright green paper soon an unrecognizable mass. When the soldier came back he fell asleep, his head lolling back, his mouth open. Dreaming, no doubt, of his girlfriend's soft arms, his mother's apple pie. Soon everyone was asleep, the carriage filled with exhaled breath while we watched through the window.

'What can we do?' I whispered to our reflections. 'What can we ever do?'

Ruth reached for my hand and we held on to each other as we moved through the country called night.

The next day the countryside was untouched by war, but still dead and colourless beneath a lowering sky. When we finally reached Bordeaux everything speeded up around us, the crowds at the station, the docks. Faces looming and receding – a woman's fat cheeks, her mouth opening and closing soundlessly, a man's bushy eyebrows, the red lines on the back of the taxi driver's neck. We were swept along, our feet so heavy we could barely put one in front of the other. The ship rearing up, impossibly huge, our hands on the grimy rope of the gangway.

Dr Maitland

Someone told me they needed my attention, and when they didn't appear at dinner I went looking, knocked at their cabin door. They were very agitated when I entered. One – I don't know which – was pacing back and forth, her hands in her hair. One was sitting at the tiny writing desk, scribbling on pieces of paper which fell to the floor as I closed the door behind me. I introduced myself, and the pacing one sat down on the edge of the bunk, folding her hands in her lap. I asked how they were and they said they were very tired, that they hadn't slept for the two days it took the train to reach Bordeaux. They said there was a terrible racket in their heads, that if they could just sleep maybe it would stop. They asked if I knew when the ship would sail, and I said that I understood that it would be within the hour. I gave them a mild sedative and said that I would come back in the morning. I've thought about it since, and I don't think there's any way I could have known. You can't imagine what it was like, the stress we'd all been living under. To be suddenly on the verge of a normal life. The cruel limbo of the sea voyage. Everyone on that ship was in distress, and I couldn't have known what they would do.

doesn't exist for them

The Deep

Without each other we are in pieces, we are scattered to the wide winds. These past weeks we are put together like the broken teacup. In the train our shoulders bumped and we felt those rough edges grating. Nothing feels as it did; we have to find a way back.

There is a terrible racket in our heads. In the cabin we pace and pace, and our hearts beat loudly, thrumming to our fingertips. We are the same age our mother was when we were born.

The doctor comes with soothing powders, but we are beyond that. She says with a smile that in a few days we'll be home again, as if that should mean something. We pace and pace, holding ourselves together. Bits of us straining to break loose; we will be scattered.

The ship moves off with a lurch and we pace and pace; we are trapped now, there's a terrible pounding in our heads. The lighthouse sends its beam through the cabin, a darting streak of light, and we know, suddenly, what we have to do.

Testimony of the Sentry

Walter Allingham, 339th Field Artillery, was stationed in the bow on Sunday night. He saw two young women walking along the deck toward him at about seven o'clock. It was so dark he could not see what they wore, except what appeared to be big cloaks which blew out in the wind. They were talking to each other and stopped when they reached the bow on the port side. Suddenly one of them placed her foot on the rail and scrambled over it, jumped into the water. The other followed almost immediately. Neither screamed or made any noise, and the splash when they struck the water was drowned by the noise of the tide rushing along the ship's sides.

After

Here there are two tall windows and the gauzy white curtains lift and fall like a breath, like a sigh. The sounds that reach us are muffled, and we wonder if someone has died.

A graduate of York University and the University of Guelph, Mary Swan has been published in numerous magazines and journals. Her stories have also been published in several anthologies including *Emergent Voices* (Goose Lane 1990), *Coming Attractions* (Oberon 1999), *Best Canadian Stories 92 (Oberon* 1992) and most recently *The O. Henry Awards Prize Stories* (2001) where 'The Deep' took First Prize.

Mary Swan has travelled extensively throughout Europe and currently lives in Guelph with her husband and daughter.